Acting Edition

1+1

by Eric Bogosian

⫼SAMUEL FRENCH⫼

No one shall make any changes in this title(s) for the purpose of production. No part of this book may be reproduced, stored in a retrieval system, scanned, uploaded, or transmitted in any form, by any means, now known or yet to be invented, including mechanical, electronic, digital, photocopying, recording, videotaping, or otherwise, without the prior written permission of the publisher. No one shall share this title(s), or any part of this title(s), through any social media or file hosting websites.

For all inquiries regarding motion picture, television, online/digital and other media rights, please contact Concord Theatricals Corp.

MUSIC AND THIRD-PARTY MATERIALS USE NOTE

Licensees are solely responsible for obtaining formal written permission from copyright owners to use copyrighted music and/or other copyrighted third-party materials (e.g. artworks, logos) in the performance of this play and are strongly cautioned to do so. If no such permission is obtained by the licensee, then the licensee must use only original music and materials that the licensee owns and controls. Licensees are solely responsible and liable for clearances of all third-party copyrighted materials, including without limitation music, and shall indemnify the copyright owners of the play(s) and their licensing agent, Concord Theatricals Corp., against any costs, expenses, losses and liabilities arising from the use of such copyrighted third-party materials by licensees. For music, please contact the appropriate music licensing authority in your territory for the rights to any incidental music.

IMPORTANT BILLING AND CREDIT REQUIREMENTS

If you have obtained performance rights to this title, please refer to your licensing agreement for important billing and credit requirements.

1+1 received its world premiere in a co-production between New York Stage and Film and the Powerhouse Theater in Poughkeepsie, NY, on July 3, 2008. The production was directed by Mark Brokaw. The cast was as follows:

BRIANNE. . . . . Kelli Garner
PHIL. . . . . Josh Hamilton
CARL . . . . Matthew Maher

On March 1, 2023, the play premiered off-Broadway at the SoHo Playhouse. The production was directed by Matt Okin. The cast was as follows:

BRIANNE. . . . . Katie North
PHIL. . . . . Daniel Yaiullo
CARL . . . . Michael Gardiner

CHARACTERS

BRIANNE – Brianne is in her mid-20s. Working as a waitress as she tries to "break into" the acting business in Los Angeles. She's attractive and energetic. She spends a lot of time checking herself out in the bedroom mirror, trying to figure out if she's pretty enough to be a model or an actress.

PHIL – Phil is in his early 30s. He wears a suit jacket but no tie. Maybe he's a fashion photographer. His good looks and style suggest that he travels widely and that he's sophisticated in some way. When we first meet him, he affects a British accent. He's smooth and easy with Brianne.

CARL – Carl manages the Steak & Brew pub. Because he's given up on his looks and his body, he no longer makes an effort. He works long hours every week, and he's not happy with his life. He is Brianne's boss and has a crush on her.

SETTING

Various locations in Los Angeles, CA.

TIME

The recent past.

AUTHOR'S NOTE

The staging of this piece should be sparse – a café table suggests the restaurant, scattered photos on the floor suggest Phil's studio, etc.

The audience should feel that they know exactly where the story is heading. When things turn in the second act, there should be absolutely no sense that either Phil or Brianne (or Carl) are in the wrong. The argument has to be perfectly balanced.

ACT ONE

Scene One

*(***BRIANNE*** *enters carrying a tray of food and drink to* **PHIL**, *who is seated at a small table reading a newspaper.)*

BRIANNE. Here you go! New York strip, baked potato with sour cream and a...Beck's. Enjoy!

(She places the items before him.)

PHIL. *(British accent.)* Thank you very much.

BRIANNE. *(Sunny, without irony.)* You're welcome! Let me know if you need anything else.

*(***BRIANNE*** *turns to go.)*

PHIL. Wow!

BRIANNE. I'm sorry, you need something?

PHIL. *(Laughing.)* No, no. I just...

BRIANNE. You sure? Steak sauce?

PHIL. No, no, it's just...nevermind, I'm being stupid.

BRIANNE. What?! Now you have to tell me!

PHIL. Well, you just said "You're welcome." And honestly, since moving to Los Angeles, I rarely hear that from anyone. No, that's not it. I *do* hear it. It's that you said it like you meant it.

BRIANNE. And that's funny?

PHIL. No, no! Well, yeah. No. Not funny...refreshing.

BRIANNE. Oh. OK. Well, just let me know if you need anything.

PHIL. I'm just saying...what am I saying? People are not nice. The humanity rubs off of people, like plate brass and all you get is the tin underneath and it's not pretty. And you are...

BRIANNE. Pretty?

PHIL. Well...yes...but I meant in a deeper way.

BRIANNE. People suck.

PHIL. Well, they can be *ugly*. You know? And I say, "why?" Why not be civilized, right? We're not crabs in a bottle. We're *people*. Each and every one of us. Right?

BRIANNE. Even waitresses.

PHIL. Especially waitresses!

    (Beat.)

BRIANNE. Where I come from we have this weird habit of saying "Please" and "Thank you" and "You're welcome."

PHIL. Where's that?

BRIANNE. What?

PHIL. Where are you from?

BRIANNE. Phoenix. Near Phoenix. Lived in Seattle for a while, then down here. And uh, you're not from LA either are you?

PHIL. Originally? London.

BRIANNE. England?

PHIL. Very good! See, you're nice *and* you're intelligent.

BRIANNE. I was just telling Carl, my assistant manager, that guy at table five is *not* American.

PHIL. I'm what you call a "resident alien." Which is a bizarre term when you think about it. Like I'm from outer space or something. You know?

BRIANNE. *(Not getting it.)* Right. *(Getting it.)* Right!

> *(Uncomfortable pause as **BRIANNE** finds herself gazing into **PHIL**'s baby blues.)*

PHIL. You know what? I *will* have some steak sauce if you've got it.

BRIANNE. Sure thing! Coming right up!

> *(**BRIANNE** exits.)*

> *(**PHIL** scans his newspaper. **CARL**, the assistant manager, passes by, giving **PHIL** the barest glance.)*

> *(**BRIANNE** reenters with the steak sauce. **PHIL** is immersed in his paper.)*

There you go.

> *(**BRIANNE** hands **PHIL** the bottle. He looks up from the paper and beams.)*

PHIL. Thank you!

BRIANNE. You're welcome!

> *(They both get the joke...)*

So what? Lemme guess, you're a producer.

PHIL. Now why on earth would you think that?

BRIANNE. Because that's what guys who are hitting on me always claim to be. You know they make small talk and then they say "I'm producing a movie! You should come by for an *audition!*"

PHIL. No! Was I hitting on you? I'm sorry.

BRIANNE. No, it's cool. I mean. Nevermind.

> *(Embarrassed,* **BRIANNE** *turns to go. But stops herself and returns to* **PHIL.***)*

See the problem is you can't tell the real producers from the fake producers. And I'm an actress, I mean I moved to LA to, you know, act. So I need to know the difference. Between the real and the fake. You know? I'm sorry.

PHIL. Apology accepted.

BRIANNE. Thanks. So, what do *you* do?

PHIL. Me? I'm...a photographer.

BRIANNE. Really? Like for, what, magazines?

PHIL. Sort of. I used to be one of those guys you see at the foot of the fashion show runways, snapping like hungry piranha. Now I mostly do studio work.

BRIANNE. No shit. Ever been to Paris?

PHIL. Paris, Milan, Berlin. Used to live out of my suitcase. But the business is run by scoundrels and freaks. And in the end, the pay isn't worth the aggravation. Lots of glitz covering up a sordid and depressing business.

BRIANNE. Don't tell me about lousy pay.

> *(***CARL*** *crosses again, upstage of where* **BRIANNE** *and* **PHIL** *are talking.)*

CARL. Brianne, when you get a chance, table six wants a refill? And three needs their onion rings.

> *(***BRIANNE*** *barely acknowledges* **CARL** *as he exits.)*

PHIL. Listen, you're working, I don't want to get you in trouble.

BRIANNE. Can I ask your opinion about something?

PHIL. Sure.

BRIANNE. You're a photographer, right? OK. Well, I need a headshot and this guy wants to charge me nine hundred bucks. You think that's cool?

PHIL. Nine hundred! For a headshot?

BRIANNE. He says that's a good price.

PHIL. He better be fucking amazing for nine hundred!

CARL. *(Offstage.)* Brianne!?

BRIANNE. *(Ignoring* **CARL.***)* It's a lot isn't it?

PHIL. What's a headshot take, forty-five minutes?

BRIANNE. I don't know. I never did one before.

PHIL. Well, I don't do headshots, specifically. But…tell you what…

BRIANNE. Yeah?

PHIL. I could. I mean…I could.

BRIANNE. Yeah?

PHIL. Tell you what. You let me keep some pictures and I'll do it for free.

BRIANNE. No, listen, that's not what I was…

PHIL. You've got a great look.

BRIANNE. Yeah?

PHIL. You do!

BRIANNE. You know, don't feel that you have to…

PHIL. What?

BRIANNE. I'm just saying… I don't want anything for free.

PHIL. No, listen, it would be a pleasure to shoot you. Or not. Either way, I just thought…

CARL. *(Offstage.)* Brianne?

BRIANNE. Shit. I'm sorry. I'm the one who brought it up, right? Ummmm.

CARL. *(Offstage.)* Bri?

PHIL. Look, I'm running late anyway. Why don't you give me my check and I'll give you this: *(He pulls out a business card, hands it to her.)* Call me tomorrow. Or not. Whatever. I'll be in. We'll work something out. Phil.

BRIANNE. Brianne. Thanks. Phil.

> (**PHIL** *strolls off.* **BRIANNE** *clears the plates and beer onto a tray.* **CARL** *follows her.)*

CARL. Is there a problem?

BRIANNE. No. Table six. Right now. I'm on it.

CARL. Tameka got them. But listen, it's very busy, Brianne.

BRIANNE. Yes. I know that, Carl. Thank you!

CARL. And when it gets busy...

BRIANNE. I know, I *know!*

CARL. So, what? That guy bothering you?

BRIANNE. No! We were just talking.

CARL. OK.

BRIANNE. A professional discussion.

CARL. OK.

BRIANNE. No offense Carl, but I don't give a shit about this job, OK? I'm an *actress.* This job is just, you know, something I have to do while I'm waiting for my life to begin.

CARL. I know. I'm sorry. For, you know, implying otherwise.

BRIANNE. That guy is a professional photographer. And he is going to take my headshot for free. You got a problem with that?

CARL. No. Of course not.

(Beat.)

Your headshot, huh? Could I get a copy? When it's done?

BRIANNE. Why in the world would you want a copy of my headshot, Carl?

CARL. Well, we could put it up on the wall. You know like when famous people eat someplace, they hang their picture up by the cash register, right?

BRIANNE. Carl, first of all, I'm not famous, *yet*. And second of all, I don't want every freak and weirdo who comes in here seeing my picture with my name on it so they can find me and track me down and stalk me and shit. It's bad enough.

CARL. Stalk you?

BRIANNE. I was on La Cienega yesterday at a stoplight and this freak in a convertible starts talking to me? Like he has a right? So I ignore him. Next thing I know he's gliding up next to me at *every* stoplight and just staring at me. Why? Why would a guy do that?

CARL. Because you're great-looking?

BRIANNE. That gives him the right to fucking follow me? Stare at me like a psycho?

CARL. But maybe he, you know, wanted to meet you?

BRIANNE. Oh, yeah, that's the way I want to meet someone! At a friggin' *stoplight*! He could be a serial killer for all I know.

CARL. Or maybe he's a lonely, nice guy who needs to talk?

BRIANNE. You're weird.

CARL. I'm just saying...

BRIANNE. Do you have any idea how fucked up it is that a person wants to *talk* to you just because of the way you *look*? I mean, *think* about it, Carl.

CARL. But then what's the point of looking good?

BRIANNE. Wow. On the outside, you're intelligent, you're sensitive. But on the inside, you're just like that guy at the stoplight. It's kind of scary. Take this!

(**BRIANNE** *hands* **CARL** *her tray. He exits.*
Then she pulls out a chair and sits.)

Scene Two

*(A downtown loft. **BRIANNE** is seated before backdrop paper. **PHIL** enters with a camera on a tripod. He fiddles with the equipment.)*

PHIL. Just relax.

BRIANNE. I've had my picture taken before.

PHIL. Right. So just be yourself.

BRIANNE. But I should warn you. I'm not very photogenic.

PHIL. You're joking, right?

BRIANNE. No. You'd never know it by looking at me. But it's true.

PHIL. You've never had your picture taken by a professional.

BRIANNE. Well, he was. He was the guy who takes, you know, the class picture at my high school.

PHIL. The what?

BRIANNE. Nevermind. *(Beat.)* You ever meet Kate Moss?

PHIL. Many times.

BRIANNE. She must be so beautiful in person.

PHIL. No more beautiful than you. In person.

BRIANNE. Right.

PHIL. Brianne?

BRIANNE. Yes.

PHIL. Turn your body so you're facing the wall? Then turn your head and look right at me. *(**BRIANNE** adjusts, doesn't get it exactly right.)* Right. Now look at me. Use your eyes. *(She does.)* Good. Now chin up a bit. Smile.

BRIANNE. This feels weird.

PHIL. I'll put on some music.

> (**PHIL** *goes off.* **BRIANNE** *nervously fiddles with her hair. Music.*[*] **PHIL** *returns, lighting a joint.*)

Here you go.

BRIANNE. What?! Now?

PHIL. C'mon. Go with the flow. Relax. I know you have it in you.

BRIANNE. It'll make my eyes red.

PHIL. One puff. To loosen you up.

> (**BRIANNE** *reaches for the joint and laughs.*)

BRIANNE. This is weirdness! Much weirdness.

PHIL. (*Incredulous.*) Why?

BRIANNE. No, I mean...

PHIL. What?

BRIANNE. I don't really know you...

PHIL. (*Focusing his camera.*) Uh-huh.

BRIANNE. Is this like a date? You and me?

PHIL. What?!!

BRIANNE. Never mind. Never mind I said that. God! Brianne, shut up!

PHIL. Hey, it's OK. (*Easy, trying to relax her.*) Hi!

BRIANNE. (*Trying.*) Hi!

PHIL. Feeling more relaxed now?

BRIANNE. No!

---

[*] A license to produce *1+1* does not include a performance license for any third-party or copyrighted recordings. Licensees should create their own.

PHIL. Tell me about your acting.

BRIANNE. My acting?

PHIL. You said you were an actress. What sort of plays have you done? Shakespeare? Shaw?

BRIANNE. *(Laughs.)* Who's Shaw?

PHIL. Ummm. Well, what did you play? In college…

> *(**PHIL** gets off three shots as **BRIANNE** answers.)*

BRIANNE. I dropped out of college. I didn't do plays in college.

PHIL. *(Busy, not really listening.)* Uh-huh.

BRIANNE. In high school we did this – oh shit, now I can't remember his name – the guy who wrote, you know, that movie about the two guys and the deaf girl…

PHIL. Mamet?

BRIANNE. Who? No.

PHIL. Stoppard?

BRIANNE. No. It was a guy who… never mind. *(Laughs.)* See, I'm stoned!

PHIL. Sam Shepard?

BRIANNE. Never mind. I can't think. You're getting me all confused. *(Laughs again.)* They make a deal to… like a bet… anyway, he wrote a play…this guy…and it… nevermind…

PHIL. I don't think I saw it.

> *(**PHIL** moves closer to **BRIANNE**, perhaps to kiss her. No, he's just reaching past her to straighten the collar of her blouse. Takes the joint from her and puts it out. He picks up his camera.)*

PHIL. You know how you were laughing just then?

BRIANNE. When?

PHIL. Just now.

BRIANNE. I guess...

PHIL. Do it again.

BRIANNE. What?

PHIL. Gimme a giggle!

BRIANNE. I can't just laugh like that!

PHIL. Of course you can! You're a "natural born actress," aren't you?

BRIANNE. This is... [ridiculous].

PHIL. OK, let's approach this from a different direction. You ticklish?

BRIANNE. Yes. Very. Very very.

> (**PHIL** *feints a move.*)

Don't!

PHIL. I will.

BRIANNE. I bite.

PHIL. I bet you do.

> (**PHIL** *catches her in the side. She is ticklish and laughs.*)

BRIANNE. Don't!!

> (**PHIL** *bluffs again,* **BRIANNE** *laughs. He snaps her picture.*)

> (**CARL** *has entered along the periphery and watches* **BRIANNE.**)

(**BRIANNE** *stands and says emphatically,*)

STOP!

(**PHIL** *exits with his camera.*)

Scene Three

(The "break room" at the Steak & Brew. **CARL** *hangs with* **BRIANNE**. *She lights a cigarette.)*

CARL. But you don't feel that way!

BRIANNE. Carl, how do you know how I feel? Since when did you become a mind reader?

CARL. Sorry.

BRIANNE. And stop apologizing all the time. It's boring.

CARL. Sorry.

(Beat.)

BRIANNE. Sex...sex isn't always about love.

CARL. But it is for most people. That's the way it should be.

BRIANNE. "Should"? Why "should"? Listen Carl, My mom's Catholic, OK? I've been dealing with all that guilt and hellfire stuff my whole life. I don't want to hear about "should".

CARL. No, but I mean sex is an intimate thing. Between two people. It should be respected. It's not just a physical thing.

BRIANNE. Sometimes, yes. Sometimes, no. You're totally putting *your* own value system on this.

CARL. But, OK, let's say you fall in love with someone...

BRIANNE. Yeah?

CARL. I feel weird talking to you about this.

BRIANNE. Why? Because I'm a woman?

CARL. No, because I'm your boss and it could be, you know, um, the sexual content of our conversation could be, uh, construed as harassment.

BRIANNE. What?!!

CARL. We're supposed to stick to work-related topics.

BRIANNE. Oh come on! I'm having a *conversation* with you Carl! We're discussing a *point*. And by the way, you're not my "boss." I hate that word. You're my *supervisor*. *Assistant* supervisor.

CARL. Still, the fact that you are voluntarily having a conversation with me about sexual, um, topics does not mean that it's not sexual harassment. I mean, as sexual harassment is *defined*. If we are going by the rule book, we should not be having this conversation.

BRIANNE. The "rule book?"

CARL. Yes. There's a whole chapter on sexual harassment. It's an important topic.

BRIANNE. I never even saw this rule book! "Rule book".

CARL. I'll get you a copy.

BRIANNE. *(Laughs.)* Carl, you are like the most straight-edge person I've ever met.

CARL. I take my job seriously.

BRIANNE. You're weird. You know that, right?

CARL. I'm just trying to...

BRIANNE. Well, stop trying...

> *(Beat.* **CARL** *doesn't want the conversation to end.)*

CARL. You don't think I'm your boss? I mean, technically speaking?

BRIANNE. No, you're not my *boss*. Because you can't make me do anything I don't want to do.

CARL. Right. So we're more like colleagues.

BRIANNE. Yeah. Colleagues. OK. Whatever. So, should I fold napkins?

CARL. No, we still have three minutes on the break.

BRIANNE. I've had enough break, I'm going back.

CARL. OK.

BRIANNE. Carl...you've got to relax.

> (**BRIANNE** *stubs out her cigarette, and steps into Phil's loft.)*

Scene Four

*(Phil's loft. **PHIL** huddles over contact sheets with a loupe, absorbed in what he's doing. **BRIANNE** enters and quietly watches for a few seconds.)*

BRIANNE. Hi.

*(**PHIL** looks up, surprised.)*

PHIL. Oh, hi! Come here! I'm very happy with these!

BRIANNE. You are?

*(**PHIL** hands **BRIANNE** the loupe and shows **BRIANNE** how to look at the images. There's a physical intimacy between them that **PHIL** takes for granted.)*

Yeah. They're kind of... wow, you're amazing.

PHIL. Not me, *you.* I'll let you in on a professional secret. Half the game is finding a great subject.

BRIANNE. Uh-huh. You're saying I'm a great subject?

PHIL. C'mon! Look! You emanate charisma. Look at yourself. Look! Brianne, my God! You're fantastic!

BRIANNE. *(Seduced.)* Yeah? ...Wait, you're like goofing on me, right?

PHIL. I'm not!

BRIANNE. "Charisma"?

PHIL. I may have my faults but I *never* lie, Brianne.

BRIANNE. You don't?

PHIL. Never.

*(**BRIANNE** returns to the sheets. Captivated.)*

BRIANNE. They do look good.

PHIL. Very good. Very, very good.

> (**PHIL** *grabs a coffee table book of Steiglitz photographs of Georgia O'Keefe. Opens it and shows* **BRIANNE** *a page.*)

You do great things with your eyes. Check these out. It's the eyes that make the difference.

> (**PHIL** *takes it back, opens another book – Weston's nudes.*)

See? Amazing, huh?

BRIANNE. Wow. What... is that her *leg*?

PHIL. Incredible, huh?

BRIANNE. She's naked.

PHIL. Well of course. It's a nude, you dummy.

> (**PHIL** *lets* **BRIANNE** *flip through the book, steps away from her.*)

It's very important that I take more pictures of you. And not just headshots and portraits.

BRIANNE. "More"?

PHIL. You're a terrific subject. Something emanates from you. You glow!

BRIANNE. *(Incredulous but digging it.)* Yeah?

PHIL. I've done this a long time, Brianne. I've worked very hard at it. It's not been easy. Not easy at all. But once in a while, you find gold.

BRIANNE. Gold? Right.

PHIL. I need to capture you, all of you. Posed, not posed. *(Beat.)* In the studio. On the street. Dressed up. Casual. In the nude.

BRIANNE. Never in a million years!

PHIL. What?

BRIANNE. I am not posing in the nude, Phil.

PHIL. Why?

BRIANNE. Duh? It's obvious.

PHIL. Not to me. You're saying "no" to something before you've even considered it.

BRIANNE. I've thought about…stuff like that…before.

PHIL. Stuff like what? I don't even know what you're talking about. Brianne, you are lovely and there's nothing wrong with that.

BRIANNE. OK, OK…whatever. But Phil, it's not that I don't trust you. It's that…you know… I don't really want naked pictures of me…you know…out there…

PHIL. Naked pictures? Brianne!

BRIANNE. Well, I don't.

PHIL. You *have* to let me shoot you again!

BRIANNE. Well, yeah. Sure. Of course.

PHIL. This is what we'll do. We'll take it one step at a time. If there's something that makes you uncomfortable, I won't pursue it.

BRIANNE. But *not* naked. I mean first of all we don't know each other that well, right? Plus, you know what? I'd be very nervous.

PHIL. Part of the job of the photographer is making the subject feel relaxed.

BRIANNE. And how would you relax me this time? Shoot me up with heroin?

PHIL. Only if absolutely necessary.

BRIANNE. *(Sarcastic.)* Hah-hah.

> **(PHIL** *touches her arm.)*

PHIL. Do you trust me?

BRIANNE. No.

PHIL. No?!!

BRIANNE. This is confusing.

PHIL. Trust me. I'm telling you to trust me.

BRIANNE. Yeah?

> *(Beat.)*

PHIL. You're such a tough cookie.

BRIANNE. MMM-hmmm.

PHIL. You know what, forget it. It's not that important. We don't have to do any more pictures.

BRIANNE. I'm not saying...

> **(PHIL** *kisses her. He leans back to gauge her reaction.)*

PHIL. Hi.

BRIANNE. Hi.

> **(BRIANNE** *kisses him back. After another kiss* **PHIL** *steps away from* **BRIANNE** *and wanders off.)*

Scene Five

*(The break room at the restaurant. **BRIANNE** on her cell phone.)*

BRIANNE. Hi it's me (...) Brianne! Your daughter! I just wanted to call and say happy birthday. (...) I dunno, Ma. Ten thirty? (...) Because I work the night shift tonight. (...) Four to midnight. (...) That's my job, Ma. (...) Of course I eat. I work in a restaurant! I eat all day. (...)Well, I haven't had any this week. But I'm going to drop off my new headshot, when I get it, to some places in Burbank and then I might get an audition. (...)Burbank, Ma! That's where casting places and studios are. Nevermind. (...) I don't know, Ma, I'm not really thinking about Thanksgiving right now. (...) Ma, please don't guilt me out right now, I just woke up. (...) Frank Wagner? Why are you bringing him up? For God's sakes, Ma! (...) *Was*, Ma. *Was*. Not *is*. *Was* my boyfriend. Jesus, Ma, what are you doing? Hanging around the Shop Rite talking about me with everybody who walks by? (...) No he wasn't! He was not. Did he tell you that? Don't say that, Ma, because it's not true. We were *not* engaged. Don't say that. (...) No. I could not have been. Never. See that's the thing. I never could be engaged to Frank or Billy or any of those morons. Because they are morons. And if I had to spend my life with morons, I would kill myself. (...) I'll talk any way I want to, Ma. Do you know what he said to me? Do you know what that *moron* said to me the night I left? Me, just trying to be nice and say goodbye on good terms and leave it like that and everything? Do you know what Frank said? He said, "You'll be back." He thinks I'm going to screw up out here. That I'm going to be sorry and come back to him with my tail between my legs. And that's not going to happen because I'm *not* sorry. Not for one second. So fuck him. Fuck Frank. (...) No I will swear like this if you keep bringing him up. (...) Look, I gotta go back to work. I just wanted to wish you happy birthday. So (…) happy birthday. (…) Yeah, me too. Bye. (**BRIANNE** *hangs up.*)

(**CARL** *has been watching her.* **BRIANNE** *lights a cigarette.*)

BRIANNE. I'm on break.

CARL. No, I'm not… I was just going to say, I got a phone number for you.

BRIANNE. Phone number?

CARL. Of a guy. I was in this coffee shop out at Venice Beach? And he was sitting at the next table reading a script? Turned out, he's a CAA agent. That's a very big talent agency.

BRIANNE. I know what CAA is.

CARL. So I told him about you and how talented you are, and he said that you should call him.

(**CARL** *hands* **BRIANNE** *a business card.*)

BRIANNE. *(Sarcastic.)* Great, thanks a lot Carl.

CARL. I thought you'd be happy.

BRIANNE. You did, huh?

CARL. You need an agent, right?

BRIANNE. Carl, listen to me. There's a right way and a wrong way to do things. And someone like me only gets so many chances. OK? *(She hands the card back to* **CARL.***)* Now, see, because you talked about me to this guy, I can't *ever* go to CAA to look for an agent. Ever, never.

CARL. Why?

BRIANNE. Because…because I can't. Because… look Carl, I know you're trying to help me, but don't, OK?

CARL. You're gonna be a star someday.

BRIANNE. See, even that. You saying that. Don't say that.

CARL. Why?

BRIANNE. It *jinxes* things, that's why! Don't be stupid, Carl! This isn't a game! Maybe you're happy working this dumb job in this dumb place, being a nobody for the rest of your life, but I'm *not*. I'm serious. I'll do what it takes. I'll make the sacrifices I have to make and take the pain I have to take. It's not some casual thing with me.

CARL. OK.

BRIANNE. I want more.

CARL. Of course. You should.

BRIANNE. Don't try to help me. I can take care of myself.

Scene Six

   (Phil's loft. The camera is set up facing an empty chair.)

   *(**PHIL** is rolling a joint.)*

PHIL. *(Shouting off.)* Brianne?

BRIANNE. *(Offstage.)* Yeah?

PHIL. You okay? You ready to shoot some more?

BRIANNE. *(Offstage.)* What?

   *(**PHIL** lights the joint.)*

PHIL. I said are you okay?

BRIANNE. *(Offstage.)* Just a minute!

PHIL. That wasn't so bad, was it?

   *(**PHIL** waits for an answer. No answer. Beat. He takes a step toward where **BRIANNE** seems to be, then thinks better of it, returns to his camera, checks it.)*

Fuck.

   (He smokes nervously.)

Bri?!

   *(**BRIANNE** appears wrapped up in a huge white robe, barefoot.)*

Hi.

BRIANNE. Hi.

PHIL. Ready to shoot a bit more?

BRIANNE. Sure.

PHIL. Oh, because...

BRIANNE. No, I just had to…you know, pee.

PHIL. Oh.

> (**PHIL** *passes the joint to* **BRIANNE**. *She takes it absent-mindedly.)*

I was going to say…

BRIANNE. What?

PHIL. That wasn't so bad, was it?

BRIANNE. No. It was fun. Exciting.

PHIL. You look great. Pictures are going to be very good.

BRIANNE. Cool.

PHIL. Light's important and I got it just right. It's the whole thing, really. Have to balance light, stock, skin tone. It's an art. And I'm good at it.

BRIANNE. I know.

PHIL. There are wankers out there, they just shoot. Blast away. OK, if you're paparazzi, that's one thing. But to get the foreground, background, the *sense* of the thing perfect, it takes skill.

> (**BRIANNE** *takes the joint.)*

BRIANNE. I pretended I was playing a part.

PHIL. What?

BRIANNE. It's like acting. For the camera. Pretending.

PHIL. Absolutely. That's it. You know, people think that beauty is something concrete. Bone structure, lips, eyes, tits. But it's much more. Much more. You can have all that, but if there's no spirit, you've got nothing. The inner vitality, that reaches out. Know what I'm saying? It takes two to tango. You send out the spirit and I catch it with my camera.

BRIANNE. So, this is like, spiritual?

PHIL. Yeah. In a way. We're making art. And you are my muse.

BRIANNE. "Muse"?

PHIL. The muses were like the goddesses of art. They inspired the great artists. That's what you'll be to me. You know?

>   (**BRIANNE** *laughs, a little stoned.*)

BRIANNE. Phil... You are so full of shit!

PHIL. I'm not!

BRIANNE. Yes you are. But it's OK. I like it.

PHIL. I know you do.

BRIANNE. I like you.

PHIL. I like you. A lot.

BRIANNE. *I* need a muse.

>   (**PHIL** *busies himself with his camera. Getting ready to shoot again.*)

PHIL. Why do you need a muse?

BRIANNE. For artistic inspiration.

PHIL. You going to start taking pictures too?

BRIANNE. No, for my work. My acting.

PHIL. You will. You will.

BRIANNE. No really, I need to. I didn't come to LA to waitress at Steak & Brew!

PHIL. Maybe you should take some classes.

BRIANNE. I don't need classes. I need an *audition*. I haven't had one since I got here.

PHIL. You haven't been here that long.

BRIANNE. Look, I think, what we're doing is, you know, cool, and it's something that you and I are doing and I like it a lot. You know that. It's just... I came here with a plan, you know? I had a plan and I was going to do my plan and it's just not going the way I hoped it would go. My plan.

PHIL. Maybe you need to adjust your plan.

BRIANNE. You don't get what I'm saying.

PHIL. Maybe you need to take your hands off the steering wheel for a minute and see what happens.

BRIANNE. Is that what you're doing?

PHIL. Maybe.

BRIANNE. You're not.

PHIL. Isn't it all about trying to stay in control? Isn't it all about right and wrong, and good and bad? You say you hate your mom. But you know who God is? Your mom in your head. Why don't you do what feels right, instead of what you think you *should* do all the time.

BRIANNE. What feels right?

PHIL. Don't be afraid to let go. Jump into the unknown.

    (**PHIL** *focuses up on her.*)

Wait, turn around. But keep looking at me.

    (**BRIANNE** *turns her back on* **PHIL,** *but turns to look at him. He snaps her picture. Then he begins to walk around her.* **BRIANNE** *has her back to the audience, so her open robe can't be seen by the audience.* **PHIL** *walks around her, snapping her.*)

Sit down. On the floor.

    (**BRIANNE** *sits on the floor.*)

PHIL. Let go of the front of your robe. Open it.

>*(She does. The audience can't see what **PHIL** can see. He snaps her picture.)*

Look up at me.

>*(Click.)*

Amazing. Brilliant. Now *look* at me.

BRIANNE. I am looking at you.

PHIL. No, really look at me. With your heart. With your soul.

>*(**BRIANNE** looks up at **PHIL**. He gives her a quick kiss and keeps shooting.)*

Look at me as if you love me. Really love me. *(Click.)* You are so beautiful. *(Click.)* My God.

Scene Seven

*(Carl's room. Lights up on **CARL**, he's staring at his laptop intently, has earphones plugged in. The laptop blocks our view of his crotch.)*

CARL. Hi, uh, Marketa. That's a great name, Marketa. What is it, Dutch? Oh. Cool. (...) It's Nick. Nicholas. My friends call me Nick. What time is it over there? Yeah, I guess that would be right. (...) Just got home from work. (...) Uh, I'm a computer programmer. Yeah, I work for Apple. Ever hear of the iPhone? Yeah, I invented the software. (...) Oh yeah. So, uh, could you, right. Yeah, that. Could you take that off? Great. Great. You have uh, great, uh, uh, how old are you? (...) Really? You seem younger. Um, (...) sure, sure, right do that. But no, no dildo. I don't like dildoes. Huh? Oh, OK. Sure if you want to. I mean only do that if you want to. (...) Well, that's good that you, uh, like me to watch because I like watching! *(Self-conscious laugh.)* Oh, my god. Marketa, you are... my god you're beautiful. And yes, yes, that's right. Could you just uh, tilt your legs, right...like that. Uh-huh. Yes. Yes. Are you...? Are you coming? Yeah? Me too... Oh. Oh. Oh. Shit! SHIT! Hello? Marketa? I lost the connection, wait a second. Fucking Time Warner, fuck-fuck-fuck!!!!

*(**CARL** tears off the earphones, tries to reconnect, can't. Gets very upset. Stands, his pants unzipped, wearing boxers. Walks around, pulls his pants up and buckles his belt.)*

I'm fucked up. I'm fucked-up. I'm fucked-up. Fuckin' loser. I'm a loser. A fucked-up loser. Me and my dick. I hate having a dick. I should cut it off. Cut it off and burn it on a sacrificial altar.

Scene Eight

> *(Phil's loft. He enters with a sheaf of eight-by-ten photos. He begins to arrange them on the floor, so he can scan them all at once.* **BRIANNE** *enters.* **PHIL** *continues to do what he's doing, talking as he goes.)*

PHIL. When I was a kid, I was an ugly duckling. Grotesque. All nose and chin. I'd ask girls out, they'd laugh at me. That's why I love beauty.

BRIANNE. I don't believe you. You were never ugly.

PHIL. Had zero confidence. Was resigned to spending my life alone, unloved.

BRIANNE. Right.

PHIL. I'm just saying... what am I saying? You either have it or you don't. Bri, you have it. It's a gift.

BRIANNE. Phil?

PHIL. Um-hmmmmmm?

BRIANNE. Where are the other pictures?

PHIL. I have them.

BRIANNE. Can I see them, please?

> *(From the sheaf,* **PHIL** *peels off a dozen photos, hands them to* **BRIANNE**. *For a moment nothing is said. Then.)*

PHIL. They are extraordinary.

BRIANNE. *(Hesitant.)* Yeah. You can almost see everything.

PHIL. I showed them to a colleague. He was knocked out.

BRIANNE. Colleague? What colleague? Who?

PHIL. Someone who knows.

BRIANNE. Someone?

PHIL. These pictures are terrific, Brianne. I couldn't keep them to myself.

BRIANNE. These were for you. Only.

PHIL. You don't like them.

BRIANNE. I didn't say that.

PHIL. I've never done such good work.

(*Beat.*)

I'm sorry you don't like them.

BRIANNE. So what did your expert friend say?

(**BRIANNE** *won't look up from the photos.*)

PHIL. He flipped.

BRIANNE. You mean jerked off.

PHIL. Maybe. But how do *you* feel about them? Do you like them? You do. I can tell you do.

BRIANNE. They're... if I didn't know they were me, I would like them, I guess. I mean, they're beautiful.

PHIL. Check out that expression in your eyes. Do you have any idea how hard that is to do?

BRIANNE. No one's going to be looking at my *eyes*.

PHIL. Marty wants to post them on his site.

BRIANNE. Oh Jesus. "Marty," is that his name?

PHIL. He said they were the best he'd seen in years.

BRIANNE. Phil, I am *naked* in these pictures.

PHIL. Brianne, for God's sake! Will you stop being such a fucking Puritan! Jesus! What is wrong with you? What year is this? Eighteen ninety-nine? You are beautiful woman. These are amazing photographs.

BRIANNE. Don't yell at me.

PHIL. Well, I have to yell if I'm going to get through to you! My God. You know, this isn't just about you and what *you* want. This is about *me* too. My work. My career. But you don't care about that.

BRIANNE. Your work is great.

PHIL. Really? Because I would never know that from the way you're acting.

BRIANNE. That's not fair.

PHIL. Fair? What's fair? That I work my ass off for fifteen years, killing myself to perfect my craft and now, now that I have made something that is brilliant, truly brilliant, I can't show it? I am denied? I thought you cared about me, about what I do.

BRIANNE. This website...it's a porn site?

PHIL. *No.* It's a *photography* site. Very serious. Very high end. Photographs of women, yes. Nude, yes. Mostly nude. But only the most beautiful women by the most *top* photographers.

BRIANNE. I love your pictures, don't say that I don't. *(Beat.)* This is really important to you, I know.

PHIL. It should be important to you too. It *is* you. It's you *and* me, something we're doing together.

> *(Beat.)*

Plus, there's one other consideration.

BRIANNE. Yeah? What's that?

PHIL. You will be paid. For the use.

BRIANNE. Use?

PHIL. People click onto your image, Marty's server registers it, the site pays. Two cents. Every time someone clicks. Every picture.

BRIANNE. Two cents?

PHIL. He cuts a check twice a month.

BRIANNE. A check. For what? Fifty cents?

PHIL. A bit more than that. You want to work in the Steak & Brew the rest of your life?

BRIANNE. You're nuts!

PHIL. True.

BRIANNE. How much do we get? Realistically?

PHIL. Two cents plus two cents plus two cents plus two cents. It adds up.

BRIANNE. Can I think about it?

(**PHIL** *takes* **BRIANNE** *in his arms. Kisses her.*)

PHIL. This will be good. You'll see. You'll thank me.

Scene Nine

*(**BRIANNE** and **CARL** are in the middle of one
of their philosophical discussions.)*

CARL. That I went over to help? Because they were
harrassing those girls! I mean these guys were complete
assholes and then next thing I know, I'm in the middle
of it and the girls are like, "It's OK. We're OK." Right?
I'm trying to help and they're like, "Don't bother us."

BRIANNE. Right.

CARL. It's my responsibility to make sure the patrons
aren't bothered. I'm *helping* them.

BRIANNE. Right.

CARL. See what I'm saying?

BRIANNE. Yeah...

(Beat.)

So what's that got to do with what I was saying about
my relationship with Phil?

CARL. Empathy. You know?

BRIANNE. Phil has empathy. He's filled with empathy. He's
just very serious about his work. Very serious.

CARL. He's a photographer.

BRIANNE. Uh-huh.

CARL. He must be very successful.

BRIANNE. He's going to be. He's smart. You'd really like him.

CARL. Yeah, I bet.

BRIANNE. And he's going to help me.

CARL. That's good.

BRIANNE. With my success.

CARL. Good.

BRIANNE. Don't get all sarcastic on me, Carl.

CARL. What?!!

BRIANNE. I hear your tone.

CARL. What tone?!!

BRIANNE. I respect you Carl. But do *not* judge me.

CARL. OK.

BRIANNE. OK.

CARL. OK.

Scene Ten

> (**BRIANNE** *turns and "walks into" the room as* **PHIL** *enters with a frothing bottle of champagne.*)

PHIL. We are celebrating!

BRIANNE. What are we celebrating?

PHIL. Look at this.

> (**PHIL** *shows* **BRIANNE** *a check as he pours out a plastic cup of champagne for her, then drinks from the bottle.*)

BRIANNE. Does that say "sixteen thousand dollars"?

PHIL. Two cents times a hundred thousand viewers clicking on your photos an average of eight times comes to sixteen thousand dollars. And that's the *second* check. I cashed the first already.

> (**PHIL** *pulls out a wad of big bills.*)

How many thousands would you like? Two, three?

> (**PHIL** *peels off some cash and hands it to* **BRIANNE.**)

BRIANNE. You should keep some.

PHIL. Don't worry about me.

> (**BRIANNE** *stares at the cash in her hand while she sips her champagne.*)

Toss it up into the air.

BRIANNE. What?

PHIL. Toss it. It's a nice feeling.

(**BRIANNE** *throws the cash in the air. They laugh.*)

More champagne, my dear?

(*They drink from the bottle and the froth makes a mess.*)

Two cents plus two cents plus two cents.

BRIANNE. Yeah…

PHIL. FUCKING THOUSANDS!!!

(*More laughing and drinking.*)

Marty wants more pictures. You're a big hit.

BRIANNE. But only for Europe, right?

PHIL. Why? You think your mom's gonna be surfing the net and see your naked bum?

BRIANNE. Not just my mom!

PHIL. Hi Mom!!!

BRIANNE. Are you drunk?

PHIL. No one will *ever* see this stuff! Even if they do, they'll never know it's *you.* That's the thing about the internet. It's so fucking huge, it's automatically anonymous. Even if someone saw you on the street two minutes after they clicked you on a website, they wouldn't be able to put it together.

BRIANNE. Just humor me.

PHIL. People think you're a schoolgirl from *Amsterdam.*

BRIANNE. And where are all these people?

PHIL. Throw in Canada and he gives us a bonus.

BRIANNE. Canada?

PHIL. It's money, Bri. And money is freedom. It lets you do whatever you want. Act. Write. Take pictures.

BRIANNE. I like money. Everyone likes money. Money cuts through the bullshit. Makes things right again.

PHIL. Yes! When you have money, you can say "Thank you and fuck you!"

BRIANNE. How 'bout if I say, "fuck you" to Marty?

PHIL. Go ahead. But take his money!

BRIANNE. And fuck you too.

PHIL. Why me?

> (**BRIANNE** *pouts.*)

Why me, Brianne? What did I do?

BRIANNE. I don't know.

PHIL. Don't fight money. Money makes you free.

BRIANNE. Money is good. Right?

PHIL. Money *is* good. Money is *very* good.

BRIANNE. I like money.

PHIL. I love money.

BRIANNE. Me, too.

PHIL. I love it almost as much as I love you.

> (*They kiss. Break apart.* **BRIANNE** *begins dialogue with* **CARL** *in next scene. Eventually,* **PHIL** *exits.*)

Scene Eleven

*(**BRIANNE** and **CARL** talking.)*

BRIANNE. I don't have to give you my reasons.

CARL. No, you don't. I'm just curious.

BRIANNE. Why?

CARL. Because I uh…care about you.

BRIANNE. See Carl, you say shit like that and you creep me out.

CARL. Well, also, um, you're a very valued employee. You'll be hard to replace.

BRIANNE. OK. OK. I'll answer you if you promise you'll drop the subject. I'm going to do something else that pays like so much more money it's ridiculous. And money is freedom. It's going to give me way more free time for my acting career.

CARL. If you need more free time I'll put you on half-shifts!

BRIANNE. Carl, I can't live on half-shifts, OK? I need to make *money*. Money solves the problem. I stay here and what, I'm gonna be a waitress for the rest of my life, so burnt-out I can't audition? No. No fucking way. I didn't come all the way out to Los Angeles so I could do the same stupid job I could be doing in Phoenix. And you can't make me. I will be an actress and I'm going to do what it takes.

CARL. OK. Don't get angry! I get it.

BRIANNE. You'll find someone else who's good.

CARL. This new job, is it like a show business job? Is that it?

BRIANNE. It's, you know, in the entertainment field.

CARL. It's not dancing is it?

BRIANNE. "Dancing"?

CARL. Some of our waitresses become dancers.

BRIANNE. You know what? Shut up! Wow. You are such an asshole!

CARL. I'm sorry. I don't know what made me come up with that.

BRIANNE. Carl! What do you think of me? God! Is that a fantasy of yours? Me, stripping?

CARL. No! I'm sorry. I'm sorry. I'm sorry. Don't be mad.

BRIANNE. Look. I'll stop by once in a while and say hi? OK?

CARL. Promise?

BRIANNE. Yes.

CARL. Good. That's good. Because, you know Brianne, it's not just about the job, I mean, now that you're not going to be here anymore, I can tell you how I feel.

BRIANNE. Carl, don't do this. Please?

CARL. OK. I. Look...if the other job doesn't work out, call me here. You can always come back. OK? Or whatever. If you need anything. OK?

BRIANNE. Sure. But it *is* going to work out and then my acting is going to work out. And then I won't have to do anything I don't want to do. I'm going to think positively. Like the guy says in this video I saw, you visualize a goal and by attraction it will come to you.

CARL. Right. It will.

BRIANNE. But only if I really want it.

CARL. So uh...bye.

BRIANNE. Yeah...

   *(Awkward hug. **CARL** walks away.)*

Scene Twelve

(Phil's loft. Loud music playing. *__BRIANNE__
wearing only an oversized t-shirt over a bra
and panties. Sits on the floor editing her
contact sheets. __PHIL__ is reading from an open
laptop.)*

PHIL. "Dear Kira – I know this sounds weird..."

BRIANNE. Not really.

PHIL. "...and I'm sure you get emails like this from millions
of admirers all over the world..."

BRIANNE. It's true.

PHIL. "...but I have to meet you. Even if it's for half a
minute..."

BRIANNE. Where is he?

PHIL. "Clinton Correctional Facility" I think they call
it Dannemora. Maximum security. Gets out in six
months.

BRIANNE. What's he in for?

PHIL. I'd assume murder. Rape. Torture. Something like that.

*(__PHIL__ packs a crack pipe, takes a hit and
passes it to __BRIANNE__. She inhales and coughs.
He turns the music up very loud. They both
laugh. Smoke more, toss heads to music.)*

BRIANNE. Oh, my fucking god!

PHIL. Yeah!

BRIANNE. Shit!

---

* A license to produce *1+1* does not include a performance license for
any third-party or copyrighted recordings. Licensees should create their
own.

PHIL. Look at this. "Dear Kira."

BRIANNE. Wait! Stop! Makes me feel guilty. Us making fun of them. They don't even know my real name.

PHIL. That's showbiz. Norma Jean/Marilyn. Brianne/Kira. You're a star. Love it.

BRIANNE. Well, I do. I do. All those guys out there thinking about me.

PHIL. Because you are the most beautiful woman in the world. Look at me. You are, you know.

BRIANNE. To you.

PHIL. To me, yes. But now to everybody. The world!

> (**BRIANNE** *shows* **PHIL** *her choices on the contact sheets.)*

BRIANNE. These six. But not this one. I hate this one.

PHIL. But you look so vulnerable there.

BRIANNE. I look like a dork.

PHIL. More? *(Indicating the crack.)*

BRIANNE. We are so nuts! I can't believe you bought *crack*!

PHIL. Why shouldn't I buy crack? Because *Time* magazine says we're going to become *drug addicts*??? Oh, no!

BRIANNE. Not just *Time* magazine. My god, I think I'm going to have a heart attack! This is actually pretty great!

PHIL. You know who becomes addicted? Losers, that's who. Poor, fucked up people. Not us. This is LA, you think we're the only successful people smoking drugs? No. What do you think they do up in those mansions? The whole *point* of being successful is to do whatever the fuck you want. To be free. To buy whatever you want, fuck whoever you want, smoke whatever you want.

BRIANNE. I think I like this shit. A lot!

PHIL. Connects the fucking dots. You know what I'm saying?

BRIANNE. Sure does. More?

PHIL. All you want.

> *(They smoke. They entwine into one another.)*

You know, not everyone gets to have this.

BRIANNE. This?

PHIL. We love our work. People love us. And we have money. We are on top of the world.

BRIANNE. Yes.

PHIL. You know why?

BRIANNE. Why?

PHIL. Because we are fucking special. Because we are the best. You and me. You and me.

BRIANNE. We're lucky.

PHIL. No. You *make* your fuckin' luck. The world is full of stupid fucking people. And you make your luck. With your brains, with your skill, with your ass. Life's a problem, you fucking solve it. It's just math. But you have to have the balls to do the math. One plus one.

BRIANNE. Equals two.

PHIL. That's right.

> *(**PHIL** fills her pipe and lights it up. Watches her as she smokes. Caresses her. Takes the pipe and kisses her. They fall back into an embrace and a twilight darkness envelopes them as music swells.)*

(They break apart and **BRIANNE** *grabs the pipe and keeps smoking.* **PHIL** *walks off.* **BRIANNE** *sits cross-legged on the floor slightly upstage, smoking and getting into the music. She begins to rock gently as she smokes.)*

Scene Thirteen

(**BRIANNE** *remains in a dim light.*)

(*Light up on* **CARL**. *He is on his hands and knees. He draws himself up onto his knees and begins to pray.*)

CARL. Please?

(*The music fades.*)

I know I'm not supposed to ask for anything. But...

(**BRIANNE** *is in her pool of light smoking and rocking back and forth.*)

You know, I'm just saying...just *asking* for a little justice.

(**CARL** *stands. Brushes off his knees. He gets out his cell phone and dials.*)

(**BRIANNE***'s phone rings. She answers it.*)

Brianne?

BRIANNE. Yeah?

CARL. It's Carl.

BRIANNE. Oh, hi.

CARL. What's up?

BRIANNE. Nothing.

CARL. Just called because I was wondering...

BRIANNE. How are you, Carl? How're the onion rings?

CARL. Good, good. How are you?

BRIANNE. Great.

CARL. Working?

BRIANNE. Oh yeah. Lots.

CARL. That's wonderful.

BRIANNE. Lots and lots.

CARL. Anything I might be seeing…?

BRIANNE. What?

CARL. Anything, you know, "Law & Order" or something?

BRIANNE. Oh, uh, no.

CARL. Oh.

BRIANNE. Going to a lot of parties. Networking. You know.

CARL. Right. That's good. You have to do that.

BRIANNE. Meeting people.

CARL. Right.

BRIANNE. How are you?

CARL. You know, same old same old. We miss you.

BRIANNE. I bet.

CARL. You should drop by.

BRIANNE. Yeah? Carl…?

CARL. What?

BRIANNE. Nothing.

CARL. What?

BRIANNE. It's stupid.

CARL. No, it isn't. What?

BRIANNE. I've been so busy, you know?

CARL. Sure.

BRIANNE. I want to stop by. See you. See Tameka.

CARL. You should. Hey, guess what? Tameka got engaged to her girlfriend.

BRIANNE. Really?

CARL. Yeah, isn't that great?

BRIANNE. Yeah, uh, Carl?

CARL. Uh, huh.

BRIANNE. You're smart. Can I ask you a question?

CARL. Sure.

BRIANNE. Did you ever do something so bad you couldn't tell anyone about it?

CARL. Is this a hypothetical question?

BRIANNE. Hypothetical?

CARL. You want me to tell you what I did?

BRIANNE. No. But…uh…you did do something, right?

CARL. Why are you asking me this? Did someone say something to you?

BRIANNE. About what?

CARL. I'm just…

BRIANNE. No it's stupid to ask you this, because you're a nice guy and you know what you think is right.

CARL. No I don't. I mean, I do. Sort of. But I get confused sometimes. You know, we all have our days, but uh… what are we talking about?

(**BRIANNE** *laughs.*)

CARL. Brianne?

BRIANNE. You're cute, you know that?

CARL. What did you just say?

BRIANNE. I miss you.

CARL. I miss you too.

BRIANNE. [-------]

CARL. Brianne?

BRIANNE. I'm here.

CARL. Maybe we should, you know, have coffee? You want to have coffee sometime?

BRIANNE. What?

CARL. You want to have coffee one time? You and me?

BRIANNE. How 'bout right now? How 'bout you come over right now and you know we just...go...somewhere... anywhere. You rescue me.

CARL. I'm...uh...I'm at work right now. I'm closing tonight. And I'm opening tomorrow. So...

BRIANNE. Right.

> (**PHIL** *enters. He's pulling on a shirt, not really paying attention to* **BRIANNE** *on the phone. We see he's carrying a video camera. He begins to shoot* **BRIANNE** *while she talks.)*

CARL. But tomorrow afternoon? Like after four?

BRIANNE. Life is so fucking weird sometimes.

CARL. Yeah. I hear you.

BRIANNE. Carl, I gotta go.

CARL. Oh. OK. Should I call you tomorrow?

BRIANNE. You're so great. I'm so glad you called.

CARL. Me too.

BRIANNE. See you soon, OK?

CARL. Yeah. OK. Tomorrow?

BRIANNE. Sure why not?

CARL. So it's a date?

BRIANNE. I really gotta go. Be good.

CARL. OK.

BRIANNE. I love you, Carl.

CARL. Yeah, I …uh…me too. Bye.

> (**BRIANNE** *hangs up. Stunned,* **CARL** *walks off.* **BRIANNE** *stands. Faces* **PHIL**, *who is videotaping her. She begins to take off her clothes as the lights fade to black.*)

ACT TWO

Scene One

(Lights up on **PHIL** *on his Blackberry behind a desk. He is dressed more "businesslike" than previously. His manner is less wolfish and more to the point. More sober. His British accent has disappeared.)*

PHIL. Yes. That would work. Yes. By early next month. Absolutely. Cool. OK. Man. Yeah. I gotta jump. Good. Good. Thanks. Alright. OK. Good.

*(***PHIL*** clicks off. Checks his watch.)*

(Calling offstage.) Traci? When my two o'clock arrives, would you send her right in, please?

*(***PHIL*** hits auto-dial.)*

Hey honey. How you feeling? Any more kicks this morning? (…) Nice. He can't wait to get out. (…) Nothing, one more meeting and then I'm done. *And* I closed the deal with the guy in Atlanta. (…) More than that. The Aruba trip *and* the birthing class. Uh-huh. Uh-huh. Just leave it to daddy.

*(***BRIANNE*** enters. She's different, more somber. Older. More makeup.)*

BRIANNE. *(Tentative.)* Hello?

(**PHIL** *holds up one finger as if to say, "One sec!"*)

PHIL. *(To phone.)* OK, honey? Listen, my appointment's here, got to run. Alright? See you tonight. We'll go out somewhere. I'm restless. Me too. OK. Bye hon.

(**PHIL** *hangs up.*)

BRIANNE. Phil?

PHIL. Hi!

BRIANNE. It *is* you.

PHIL. Uh-huh. Sorry to be so...

BRIANNE. When I got the call from... what's her name?

PHIL. Traci.

BRIANNE. Right. I thought, can't be. But then, you know, there was no other explanation.

PHIL. I wanted to see you, face-to-face, when we, uh, talked. And I was afraid you'd hang up on me, so I had Traci...

BRIANNE. Sure. Well, here I am.

PHIL. And here *I* am. *(Beat.)* Hey.

(**PHIL** *begins to walk toward* **BRIANNE** *as if to embrace her.*)

BRIANNE. Hey.

(**BRIANNE** *walks away from him.*)

PHIL. My god! Look at you!

BRIANNE. Look at *you.*

PHIL. Oh right. Suit and tie. Never thought you'd see the day? Well, you can't beat 'em you join 'em. Funny huh?

BRIANNE. Nice office.

PHIL. They do what they can to keep me happy. I'm a big earner.

BRIANNE. I bet.

PHIL. Wow. Sit down, sit down.

(She doesn't.)

BRIANNE. Can I smoke?

PHIL. Uh, actually, no. We can go out somewhere if you want. Although, I'm not sure where actually, I never leave the office, I think there's a little café and you could smoke outside…

BRIANNE. No, that's OK. I'll just bite my fingernails.

PHIL. You look awesome.

BRIANNE. Do I?

PHIL. The beautiful girl has become the beautiful lady.

BRIANNE. Yeah. You too.

PHIL. I've become a beautiful lady?

BRIANNE. *(Sarcastic.)* Yeah.

(Pause.)

PHIL. *(Calling offstage.)* Traci? No calls. Could you close the outer door? *(To* **BRIANNE.***)* How 'bout coffee? Water?

BRIANNE. I'm OK.

(Silence.)

PHIL. How long has it…?

BRIANNE. Five years.

PHIL. Not five years….

BRIANNE. Five whole years. And one month.

PHIL. Shit.

BRIANNE. Phil...

PHIL. Yes?

BRIANNE. You...you're...you don't sound the same.

PHIL. A lot has changed, Brianne. More than you know.

BRIANNE. No but I mean...what happened to your accent?

PHIL. My accent. Oh! *(Laughs.)* I lost it.

BRIANNE. You mean, you dropped it?

PHIL. Five years ago, I was a different person... I... You can't blame me for trying to be something I wasn't. Everyone does that.

BRIANNE. Sure. Life moves on. You drop things.

PHIL. Things change. That's all.

BRIANNE. Except some things don't change. Ever. Some things are permanent.

PHIL. *(Not getting her point.)* I guess...

BRIANNE. Like our pictures? They never go away. Still out there, floating around the internet.

PHIL. Oh, I know! Isn't that funny? I mean, the last time I looked.

BRIANNE. Last time...?

PHIL. I visit the sites. I even get, uh, royalties every now and then. But you know that, I sent... you got the checks I sent?

BRIANNE. *(Measured.)* No.

PHIL. Oh, I better be sure I have the right address. I sent them to the old... well, we'll straighten it out.

BRIANNE. Can't fucking wait.

PHIL. If you're going to be angry at me Brianne, this is…

BRIANNE. Why would I be angry?

PHIL. I detect anger in your voice.

BRIANNE. I'm happy to see you Phil. Sort of unexpected, this uh, reunion. Got a letter from a brokerage. Call "Traci." Traci sets up an "appointment." All very mysterious. For a minute or two, I thought maybe you died or something.

PHIL. No, I didn't die. Far from it.

BRIANNE. In traffic sometimes, I'll look around, thinking, Phil might be in one of those cars. Or I'll be filling the tank, you know, just standing there, and thinking, what if Phil drove up right now? What would I say to him?

PHIL. Well, here I am.

BRIANNE. You never did leave Los Angeles, did you?

PHIL. Well, for a while I lived in Kauai. That's in Hawaii. I met my…uh, wife, Janice, there.

BRIANNE. Uh-huh. "Janice." That's a nice name.

PHIL. We've been married three years this, uh, next month.

BRIANNE. Cool. Kids?

PHIL. Not yet. Third trimester. Any day now.

BRIANNE. Wow. A kid.

PHIL. Yeah, me with a kid, huh?

BRIANNE. You with a kid. *(Beat.)* I'm not angry at you Phil. Not now. I was.

PHIL. Of course.

BRIANNE. For a long time.

PHIL. Yeah.

BRIANNE. A long, long time.

PHIL. Yeah.

BRIANNE. In fact, it's weird that you found me when you did. Because lately I've been trying to, you know, get on the other side of it. And then, boom, out of the blue! "Traci" calls!

PHIL. Well, yeah. Me too.

BRIANNE. It was...*you* were, a big thing for me.

PHIL. I know. Me...me too.

BRIANNE. You too, what?

PHIL. I mean to say, you were a big thing for me, too.

BRIANNE. In what way was I a "big thing"?

PHIL. As a relationship, as a person in my life. I mean we were together for almost a year.

BRIANNE. But honestly Phil, I was just an opportunity, right? An adventure.

PHIL. We were *friends*, Brianne.

BRIANNE. Were we?

PHIL. Very much. Of course!

BRIANNE. Well then, I have a question I've wanted to ask you for five years: How does a friend just disappear the way you did?

PHIL. I was fucked up. You know I was fucked up.

BRIANNE. I was fucked up too. I didn't run away from *you*.

PHIL. It wasn't *you* I was running away from. It was everything. I owed money to dealers, bookies, sharks. People were looking for me. I was fucked. Look, we're getting way ahead of ourselves here, the reason I called you was...

BRIANNE. I can guess why you called.

PHIL. You can?

BRIANNE. You're probably in some kind of twelve-step program, now. And you have a sponsor or something and...

PHIL. Bri, I'm a coke addict, alcohol addict. I mean I *was*, an addict, Brianne. And, this, OK, this is hard to say, "*sex* addict." Along with a million other things. Dude, I've even quit smoking.

BRIANNE. Don't call me "dude".

PHIL. I'm just *saying*, I understand that now. That I was a total dick. And I was wrong. And it's important that I tell you that I know I was wrong.

BRIANNE. Isn't all that twelve-step stuff some kind of spiritual thing? I thought you were an atheist?

PHIL. I have redefined God for myself.

BRIANNE. Oh, *good.*

PHIL. You're mocking me.

BRIANNE. No. I'm happy for you. So, you want to "make amends", I bet.

PHIL. Yes. I do.

BRIANNE. OK. So here I am. Amend away.

(*Beat.*)

PHIL. I'm sorry. For...taking advantage of you. You were innocent. Naïve.

BRIANNE. Uh-huh.

PHIL. I should have been more considerate. I should have warned you in some way. Told you about the others. Except, honestly, Brianne, I don't know what I would have done differently. I was obsessed with you. Intensely. No, wait, I'm lying. I knew exactly what I was doing. But you have to believe me that I thought what was happening was good for both of us. I did. In my own twisted way. I was sick. Can you forgive me?

BRIANNE. I don't blame you for any of that.

PHIL. You don't?

BRIANNE. I was obsessed with you too. Obviously. And if I didn't want my picture taken, I could have said so.

PHIL. Yes. That's right! It makes me feel so much better that you see it that way.

BRIANNE. But still, you fucked me over, Phil. You *left*.

PHIL. I was in a bad place.

BRIANNE. We heard that already.

PHIL. I had to straighten my shit out.

BRIANNE. [......]

PHIL. You know what I'm saying?

BRIANNE. You never checked in on me. You never called to ask me how I was doing. Not even one phone call.

PHIL. I wanted to, many times. And I almost did. But I was such a mess and I was trying to get my shit together. And (**PHIL** *tears up.*) I'm sorry. I'm sorry, Brianne. I never wanted to hurt you.

BRIANNE. You are sorry?

PHIL. I said I was.

BRIANNE. And you mean this? From the bottom of your heart?

PHIL. Yes!

BRIANNE. Are you crying? You're not crying!

PHIL. Brianne! What do you want me to say?

BRIANNE. Words are cheap.

PHIL. Brianne, you want me to admit I was an asshole, OK, I was an asshole. I was…irresponsible. I was…sick. But I'm getting better. And I'm allowed that, all right? OK, yes, I made other people suffer. But *I* was suffering too. So I came to a crossroads and it was either change my ways or fucking die.

And I changed. I did. I have a completely different way of going about my life now. And I live life. Really live it. I don't think about how I look or how much money I have or who I'm fucking. I live my life with love as my most important value, and I know this is going to sound hokey, but I try to "be of service".

And you can be angry. Be angry. I deserve it. But I'm not the Phil you met when you were a waitress. I'm not. I'm a new person. I quit the drugs, dropped the bullshit accent, and sold all my cameras. I started over.

And I want to be able to look everyone in the eye and be straight with them and not lie and not hurt anyone. And, you know what? I'm *doing* that. One day at a time. And….and I need to make amends. Make fun of it if you want, but that's what I need to do and that's what I'm doing. So here we are. And I'm standing before you asking you to let it go.

BRIANNE. And then everything will be alright?

PHIL. No. But better. Than it was.

BRIANNE. We'll be friends again?

PHIL. Yes. In a way. Not like before.

BRIANNE. Why not "like before"? What's wrong with "before"? Before was good wasn't it?

PHIL. Yes, of course it was good. It was amazing.

BRIANNE. So if it was amazing then, why not now?

PHIL. Jesus, I'm *married* Brianne.

BRIANNE. Your wife, uh, "Janice," wouldn't understand?

PHIL. I seriously doubt it.

BRIANNE. Then you'd have to make amends to her, too.

(**BRIANNE** *approaches* **PHIL.**)

PHIL. Don't.

BRIANNE. Don't come too close?

PHIL. You know what I'm saying.

BRIANNE. I thought you wanted to make amends?

PHIL. Brianne, look, I still find you very, very attractive.

BRIANNE. Oh, that's good. Because I still find you very, very attractive.

(**BRIANNE** *touches the lapels of* **PHIL***'s jacket.*)

I think about you. Inside me.

PHIL. I think about that...too. More than that.

BRIANNE. How perfectly we fit together.

PHIL. We did that. It's true.

BRIANNE. So...you still feel that way?

PHIL. Brianne, please sit down.

BRIANNE. Kiss me. Just once.

(**PHIL** *says nothing.* **BRIANNE** *leans forward. They kiss. The kiss evolves into something more.* **PHIL** *breaks it off and walks away.*)

That wasn't so bad, was it?

PHIL. Please?

BRIANNE. Touch me.

PHIL. No.

BRIANNE. I thought you wanted to make amends?

PHIL. This is not the way.

BRIANNE. No?

PHIL. You're fucking with me!

  (Beat.)

BRIANNE. Did you tell Janice about us?

PHIL. She knows I had another life. That I used cocaine, that I slept around...

BRIANNE. "Slept around"! You mean, "pimped"?

PHIL. No. I don't mean that.

BRIANNE. Does she know that you used to shoot porn?

PHIL. It wasn't porn.

BRIANNE. It wasn't.

PHIL. It was adult material.

BRIANNE. Does Janice like "adult material"?

PHIL. No.

BRIANNE. No? Do you cum on her face? Do you videotape her sucking your cock?

PHIL. Never.

BRIANNE. Nice girl.

PHIL. Yes. She is.

BRIANNE. OK, OK. But tell me one thing, I have to know, just between you and me, do you screw Janice in the ass?

PHIL. She's not into anal.

BRIANNE. Because I was thinking we could do a threesome! You'd like that, wouldn't you? She could lick my pussy while you take her from behind. That would be good, wouldn't it?

PHIL. You're crazy.

BRIANNE. Did you meet Janice in Cokeheads Anonymous or whatever it's called?

PHIL. I don't want to talk about Janice. This isn't about Janice.

BRIANNE. No, this is about wiping the slate clean. Wiping it all away. Wiping me away.

PHIL. I have a right to this. I've worked hard to get it all back together. You don't know how hard I worked, Brianne.

BRIANNE. And what do I have a right to, Phil?

PHIL. The same. More.

BRIANNE. Oh yeah?

PHIL. Of course. If you want it badly enough.

BRIANNE. That easy, huh?

PHIL. Not easy. Not easy at all.

BRIANNE. You've been through a lot, huh, Phil?

PHIL. Yes. I have.

BRIANNE. So now that you've said it, everything's OK again, huh? You can go back to your new life with Janice with a clean conscience. That's the point of all this right? To a clean house so you can raise your new family?

PHIL. No.

BRIANNE. Yes.

PHIL. I wanted to make things right with you.

BRIANNE. Me? Me? What do you know or care about me?

Since I walked through that door, you haven't asked me one thing about *my* life? About how *I* am.

PHIL. This whole meeting has caused a lot of anxiety for me. I apologize for being so self-centered.

(**BRIANNE** *laughs.*)

Don't laugh at me.

BRIANNE. Oh, fuck you, Phil! Don't play that Mr. Humble game with me. You always were a piece of shit, you're *still* a piece of shit and you will *always* be a piece of shit. You can "make amends" all fucking day, you're still the most selfish prick I've ever known. Ever.

PHIL. I can't help it if you're still in love with me, Brianne.

(**BRIANNE** *takes one long stride toward* **PHIL** *and slaps him hard across the face.*)

BRIANNE. Shut up! Shut your big fat fucking lying face you selfish bag of dog shit!

(**BRIANNE** *backs off and catches her breath. Rubs her hand.*)

Asshole!

PHIL. Did you hurt your hand?

BRIANNE. All this "amends stuff" – this is just for you. You don't care about me. If I dropped off the face of the earth tomorrow, you'd be so, so happy. You would.

PHIL. This isn't working. Maybe we should call it a day...

BRIANNE. No. We're not "calling it a day." We're not calling it a day. We're not done with the *amends*.

(*Long beat.* **PHIL** *tries a cooler tone.*)

PHIL. So, what *have* you been doing? Since then. Acting?

BRIANNE. Acting?!!!

PHIL. Your work.

(**BRIANNE** *laughs.*)

BRIANNE. You were always a better actor than me, Phil.

PHIL. Just tell me what you've been doing without the embellishments of resentment.

BRIANNE. Do you want to know? Really want to know? Because it's a lot, Phil. It's a fuck of a lot.

PHIL. I am genuinely curious.

BRIANNE. I bet you are. Because deep down, you're just a little kid with a pack of matches. Aren't you? Lighting fires and watching the pretty flames. Watching everything burn down. And then running away and crying and saying you're sorry.

PHIL. I'm listening.

BRIANNE. Well, let's see. One day, I woke up and my boyfriend was gone. Along with all my connections and my money and my life. I cried. A lot. Tried to figure out what to do. I had no choice. I got clean.

PHIL. Getting clean is hard.

BRIANNE. Don't tell me what's hard!

PHIL. So you're clean? Now? From everything?

BRIANNE. I had a slip. But I'm back.

PHIL. When was the last time you got high?

BRIANNE. That's not important.

PHIL. It is.

BRIANNE. Shut up and listen to me. You left. I got clean. And then I discovered...I was pregnant.

PHIL. Shit. Who?

BRIANNE. Who? Who? Who the *fuck* do you think? Who the fuck do you think? Your going-away present to your old girlfriend.

PHIL. That's not possible.

BRIANNE. How do you know what's possible? That last month...we were barely conscious...

> (**PHIL** *has no answer to this. It's true.*)

I couldn't...kill it. Her. I thought, "I'm such a horrible sinner, I'm gonna kill my baby too?" Anyway, I *wanted* her in my life. I thought this baby will keep me company and help me stay straight. And she did that.

> (**BRIANNE** *holds back tears.*)

I had to tell my mom. She told me to move back to Arizona. Can you imagine? After all I'd done? To spend the rest of my life in that prison, with my mother watching me, telling me I ruined my life? Yeah, right. So what was I going to do? Go back to Steak & Brew and waitress? Nah-uh. Live off my photo royalties? They were gone. And then a solution presented itself. I heard about these "get-togethers." Flat rate. You show up and party with guys and go home with fifteen hundred bucks. No taxes. Cash on the barrelhead.

PHIL. Brianne –

BRIANNE. Oh *yeah*. It started like that. Parties. Then trips to Vegas. "Junkets" they call 'em. And more parties and then straight-up one-on-ones. Some guys really pay the big bucks. The bills got paid. Life goes on.

> (**BRIANNE** *rummages in her pocketbook, removes a photo and hands it to* **PHIL**.)

That was taken on her fourth birthday party. Just three months ago. She's beautiful, huh?

PHIL. She's beautiful. Just like her mom.

BRIANNE. No, Phil. *No*. You can't get over on me with this one. This is a *fact*. FACT. That's your biological daughter in that photo. *Yours*.

PHIL. God.

BRIANNE. How you going to "make amends" to *her*, Phil?

PHIL. I will. I promise.

(**BRIANNE** *blows her nose, cleans up.*)

BRIANNE. Yeah?

PHIL. So you're still using? Off and on?

BRIANNE. None of your business.

PHIL. Using drugs around this baby?

BRIANNE. Shut the fuck up!

PHIL. I will give you some money.

BRIANNE. "Some" money? How 'bout *a lot* of money. Every month.

PHIL. Brianne, my means are limited. I have a family of my own.

BRIANNE. This is a paternity situation here, big guy. *Comprende*?

PHIL. What?

BRIANNE. Pa-ter-ni-tee.

PHIL. No. Do not go there.

BRIANNE. Where? Where am I going Phil? Where am I going that you didn't take me by the hand and lead me to?

PHIL. No one told you to have that baby, Brianne.

BRIANNE. "That baby" is *your* baby. *Your* daughter. Fucker. You didn't even ask me her name. You *fucker*. You piece of shit fucker. I'll take you to court and I'll string you up by your big hairy balls.

PHIL. Oh, fuck this. This is bullshit.

(*Beat.*)

BRIANNE. Now what, Phil? You want me to go? Or do you want me to stay? Or do you wanna make a deal?

 (Beat.)

PHIL. You try to put this on me. But it's not me, Bri. It's *you*. You think I didn't know you were on heroin? I knew. Of course I knew. It freaked me out because I thought it was my fault. My whole life I could fix anything I set my mind to. But I couldn't fix this. I was between a rock and a hard place. And…and…I know you're not going to believe me, but I *loved* you, Bri. So for your own good…and mine, I left. We had something, *together*, and that something was over. That's all.

BRIANNE. Not over.

PHIL. Yes. Over then. Over now. I'm sorry.

BRIANNE. Uh-huh? You think…you think you can say, "I loved you" and that's what? Gonna change things? No. NO!

PHIL. Wait a minute! Everybody breathe for a second.

BRIANNE. No.

PHIL. Brianne. Listen to yourself. You're being irrational.

BRIANNE. I'll show you irrational.

PHIL. Don't push me into a corner, Bri. Don't.

BRIANNE. You ruined my life! You have to make things right!

PHIL. But money won't do that!

BRIANNE. Fuck you. I will fuck you up.

PHIL. Wait. Wait. Stop. Stop talking. *Think*. You're an *addict*. Bri! Jesus. Come on. Don't threaten me. You don't want to threaten me. You're a *prostitute*. You're still using drugs. I can tell.

BRIANNE. That has nothing…

PHIL. You are...still...using...drugs.

BRIANNE. [--------]

PHIL. So...come on, walk through this with me. You have no money, no resources. You're one step away from being homeless. And I can't fix that. I can't fix you. There isn't enough money in the world to do that. I invited you up here today because I wanted to make things right, and you spring all this on me.

BRIANNE. I will go to court.

PHIL. No.

BRIANNE. Yes. I want a major settlement. You wrecked my life, I will wreck yours. *(Beat.)* I'll call Janice.

PHIL. Don't say that. You don't wanna say that.

BRIANNE. I will. I will call her. I don't care.

PHIL. You're backing me into a corner here.

BRIANNE. What am I supposed to do, Phil?

PHIL. What am I supposed to do? Support you and a kid? I can't do that. I *won't*.

BRIANNE. No. NO! Fuck that. Fuck that! Phil... motherfucker!

> (**PHIL** *adopts a kindly tone.*)

PHIL. Listen, I feel for you but I have a new family. An unborn son. And I will protect him with everything I can get my hands on, no matter how much I once loved you. I'm going to say this once and I'm not going to repeat myself. You have no resources. I have *all* the resources. Lawyers. "Friends." "Friends of friends." *Cops.* People who will stand like a wall of stone between you and me. Like fire.

BRIANNE. You don't know what I can...

PHIL. I offered you some money. And I will make good on that offer. And I made my amends whether you think they're bullshit or not. So, I am not guilty. Uh-uh. I suggest you accept both the cash and the apology. Because if you don't…then honestly, I feel I don't owe you a thing.

BRIANNE. Phil!

PHIL. No. I'm not paying for what you've done to yourself.

BRIANNE. *(Composing herself.)* You're bluffing.

PHIL. You're threatening me. You're forcing me. No. No. I'm sorry. You made this bed. *You.* Not me. It's you who has to lie in it.

(Calling offstage.) Traci, I'm done for the day.

*(**PHIL** hands **BRIANNE** a business card.)*

This is my lawyer's number. Call him and he will arrange some money. *Don't* call me. I mean it.

(He starts out. Stops.)

(Bemused.) You know, it's funny, you were the one who wanted your picture taken. You started this. You're lucky I'm giving you anything at all.

*(**BRIANNE** stares at the card. She takes the photograph of her daughter off his desk. Sits.)*

Scene Two

> (**CARL** *enters. He's carrying a large Starbucks take-out coffee.*)

CARL. How did it go? Where's the little one...?

BRIANNE. She's next door with Judy. *(Beat.)* It went alright.

CARL. You sure?

BRIANNE. Yes.

> *(Beat.* **CARL** *puts his coffee down carefully.)*

CARL. He asked you to forgive him?

BRIANNE. Yes.

CARL. Did you show him the picture?

BRIANNE. Yes.

CARL. Did he get upset?

BRIANNE. In a way.

CARL. Is he going to give you the money?

BRIANNE. I don't know. Yes. I guess. I don't care.

CARL. You don't *care?*

BRIANNE. He said some things.

CARL. Of course he said some things. That's how he gets what he wants. He's a con man. *(Beat.)* What kind of things?

BRIANNE. He said it was also my fault.

CARL. Your fault.

BRIANNE. He said I was, you know, thought of myself as a victim, that I did everything because I wanted to. That I screwed up because I wanted to. That it was all my fault. What happened.

CARL. That's nuts!

BRIANNE. He said he would give me some money. But not what I want. Not enough. Some. Not enough.

CARL. Brianne, this is fucked up.

BRIANNE. I know.

CARL. I mean, I don't make enough money to keep this situation going. Supporting you and your daughter. I mean, Brianne, she has to start school pretty soon. All that.

BRIANNE. I can go make some money.

CARL. No, you can't do that anymore.

BRIANNE. I'm sorry.

CARL. He owes you!

BRIANNE. I don't know. I guess. Or not. I don't know.

CARL. So where does that leave everything?

BRIANNE. Look, I'll leave if you want. *We'll* leave. You don't have to take care of us. I don't expect you to.

CARL. I don't want you to leave.

   (Pause.)

BRIANNE. I appreciate everything you've done, Carl.

CARL. Yeah?

BRIANNE. Yeah.

CARL. Wow, I'm really upset here.

BRIANNE. I know.

CARL. This guy. This guy.

BRIANNE. I know.

CARL. And seeing him again. You seeing him. Did you feel anything. For him?

BRIANNE. Carl.

CARL. No. Did you?

BRIANNE. Don't.

CARL. You did. Didn't you? Your heart went flippity-flop.

BRIANNE. Stop. I've had a hard enough day!

CARL. Did you kiss him?

BRIANNE. Carl.

CARL. This guy. This *creep*, who did all of this to you and now won't even…won't even take care of…the mess he's made. On top of that…you still have a thing for him. Fuck. And I, here I am, the fucking jerk, cleaning up… cleaning up his mess. Fuck.

BRIANNE. Carl, you've been so good to me. To us.

CARL. Fucking chump.

BRIANNE. No. You're not.

CARL. Yes.

> (**BRIANNE** *goes to* **CARL**, *stands behind him, touches him.*)

BRIANNE. I owe you so much. Without you, I would have been so lost. So lost.

CARL. You always say that.

BRIANNE. I mean it.

CARL. Don't start telling me how much you appreciate me.

BRIANNE. But I do!

CARL. Right.

BRIANNE. I do.

CARL. You say it but you don't mean it.

BRIANNE. I do mean it.

CARL. But not in the way...

BRIANNE. What?

CARL. You know what. Never mind.

BRIANNE. Carl.

CARL. If a person has to ask for love, then it's not the same.

BRIANNE. You can ask.

CARL. No. Listen. You stay here. For now. You can stay here.

BRIANNE. Shhhhhhh.

(*Beat.*)

CARL. You and your daughter mean so much to me.

BRIANNE. I know.

CARL. And I don't mean anything to you.

BRIANNE. That's not true.

CARL. Yes. It is.

(**BRIANNE** *remains behind* **CARL.**)

BRIANNE. Let me show you.

CARL. Huh?

BRIANNE. Let me show you. How I feel.

CARL. No. (*Long pause.*) It's OK. Maybe tomorrow.

(**CARL** *moves away from her, picks up his coffee, sips it. His hand is shaking. He spills coffee on himself.*)

Shit! Man... I just bought this...

(**BRIANNE** *rushes to him, tries to wipe the stain.*)

BRIANNE. It's OK, it's OK.

CARL. It's ruined. Never mind.

(**BRIANNE** *breaks away from* **CARL.**)

BRIANNE. FUCK!

(**BRIANNE** *gets out her phone. Dials.*)

CARL. Who are you calling?

(**BRIANNE** *is listening.*)

BRIANNE. Hello? Is this Janice? My name is Brianne? I'm a friend of Phil's? Your husband? Phil? (...) Philip, OK, Philip. Well, I'm a friend of his, I mean, I *used* to be a friend of his and I think you and I should talk (...) can we meet (...) What? Yes (...) yes (...) (*Long pause.*) Yes, that's right, but we should (...) oh (...) but you don't know (...) you don't (...) oh (...) you're (...) you're (...) no, but listen, you're making a mistake (...) he's (...)

(**BRIANNE** *looks at the phone.*)

She hung up on me.

CARL. Who was that?

BRIANNE. She said she already knew. That she didn't care. That she forgave him.

CARL. You called his wife? You did it? Brianne!

BRIANNE. She said "I'm not making a mistake, *you* made a mistake." She said that. Bitch. Cunt.

(**BRIANNE** *dials again.* **CARL** *takes the phone from her.*)

CARL. No. It's over Brianne.

BRIANNE. It's *not* over. It's never over. What the fuck do you know? You were born a sucker. You never wanted anything, never wanted to be anything. I'm not that. I'm not that. Fuck him. No.

(**BRIANNE** *tries to get the phone off* **CARL**. *He pushes her and she falls down.*)

You know what? Fuck you too. Fuck you. Fuck all of you. But especially *you*. Fucking boy scout. You *are* a fucking chump. Fucking boy scout. Fuck you!

CARL. You're upset.

BRIANNE.   No. No. It doesn't work that way, Carl. "Understanding" is bullshit. It's for chumps like you. For suckers. Phil was right. Everything he did was right. That's all. Fuck you. Fuck everybody.

(**BRIANNE** *storms out.* **CARL** *picks up the coffee cup and not sure where to put it, throws it against the wall.*)

(**CARL** *at a loss, sets the next scene by bringing out the café table. Bringing out the chair. Etc.*)

Scene Three

> (**PHIL** *enters and sits as he did in the first
> scene, with his beer.*)
>
> (**CARL** *approaches* **PHIL**'*s table.*)

CARL. How's everything this evening?

PHIL. Good, good. Uh...

CARL. Sir?

PHIL. Nothing.

CARL. Is something wrong?

PHIL. No... I just, I was hoping to run into someone who used to work here.

CARL. Who?

PHIL. What?

CARL. Who was it who used to work here?

PHIL. Her name was Brianne... Brianne was her name. Waitress.

CARL. Brianne. That was a while ago.

PHIL. Yes.

CARL. Six years ago.

PHIL. Yes. You know what happened to her?

CARL. Well, gee, she wasn't here very long.

PHIL. But you remember her.

CARL. Oh, sure, I just started here. I manage the place now. Used to work shifts. Now I don't have to do that. I just drop by and keep an eye on things. Six years ago...

PHIL. Yeah.

CARL. Why you looking for Brianne?

PHIL. Actually, it's funny, I owed her some money. And she never collected it.

CARL. Must have been a lot of money.

(**CARL** *is figuring it out.*)

PHIL. No... Not that much.

CARL. I see.

PHIL. You can't trace her? Find her?

CARL. Brianne?

PHIL. Brianne.

CARL. Uh...no. Can't help you there.

(Beat.)

PHIL. Well. Can't say I didn't try. Say, could you ask the waitress to get my check? I'm running late.

CARL. *(Sharply.)* Tameka! Check!

(Beat.)

I'm Carl.

(**CARL** *extends his hand.* **PHIL** *takes it.*)

PHIL. Phil.

CARL. She'll be right with you. *Phil.*

PHIL. Thanks.

(**CARL** *doesn't leave* **PHIL**'s *side.* **PHIL** *ignores* **CARL.**)

CARL. Married?

PHIL. Hmmm? Yeah.

CARL. *(Beat.)* Kids?

PHIL. Actually, we just had our first last year.

CARL. Really? That's interesting.

    (**CARL** *pulls out his wallet. Flips out a photo.*)

My daughter.

    (**PHIL** *glances at the photo with no great
interest.*)

PHIL. Pretty.

    (**CARL** *watches* **PHIL***'s reaction.*)

CARL. Yeah. She is. She'll be five in December. Great kid.

PHIL. I bet.

CARL. I love her with all my heart.

PHIL. Yeah. I know what you mean.

CARL. Her mom…her mom passed away about six months
ago.

PHIL. *(Heartfelt.)* God, I'm sorry to hear that.

CARL. Yeah. Well. Drugs. You know. Overdose.

PHIL. That's terrible.

CARL. Yeah. But life goes on. At least I have my little girl.

    (*Pause. Nothing more to say.*)

Your waitress will be right over.

    (**CARL** *steps away.*)

PHIL. Thanks.

CARL. What's that?

PHIL. I just said, "Thanks."

CARL. Oh. You're welcome. Or should I say, "Thank *you!?*"

*(**CARL** walks off leaving **PHIL**. **PHIL** takes a sip
from his beer, looks around expectantly, as –)*

(Blackout.)